ng starts here!

way and at his or her own speed. Some go back and forth between reading levels and read favorite books again and again. Others read through each level in order. You can help your young reader improve and become more confident by encouraging his or her own interests and abilities. From books your child reads with you to the first books he or she reads alone, there are I Can Read Books for every stage of reading:

SHARED READING

Basic language, word repetition, and whimsical illustrations, ideal for sharing with your emergent reader

BEGINNING READING

Short sentences, familiar words, and simple concepts for children eager to read on their own

READING WITH HELP

Engaging stories, longer sentences, and language play for developing readers

READING ALONE

Complex plots, challenging vocabulary, and high-interest topics for the independent reader

I Can Read Books have introduced children to the joy of reading since 1957. Featuring award-winning authors and illustrators and a fabulous cast of beloved characters, I Can Read Books set the standard for beginning readers.

A lifetime of discovery begins with the magical words **"I Can Read!"**

Visit www.icanread.com for information
on enriching your child's reading experience.

I Can Read® and I Can Read Book® are trademarks of HarperCollins Publishers.
Trash Truck: Meet Hank
Copyright © 2021 Netflix, Inc.
All rights reserved. Printed in the United States of America.
No part of this book may be used or reproduced in any manner whatsoever without written permission except
in the case of brief quotations embodied in critical articles and reviews. For information address
HarperCollins Children's Books, a division of HarperCollins Publishers, 195 Broadway, New York, NY 10007.
www.icanread.com

Library of Congress Control Number: 2021941535
ISBN 978-0-06-316212-9

21 22 23 24 25 LSCC 10 9 8 7 6 5 4 3 2 1 ❖ First Edition

Trash Truck
Meet Hank

By Angie Sun
Based on the Trash Truck series
created by Max Keane

HARPER
An Imprint of HarperCollins Publishers

This is Hank.

Hank is six years old.

Hank lives in a small
town with his mom, dad,
and little sister.

Hank has fun doing
anything he can imagine.

He likes to play with toys,
draw, and explore.

But Hank's favorite thing
to do is play with his best
friend, Trash Truck.

Trash Truck's favorite thing to do is collect garbage and play with Hank.

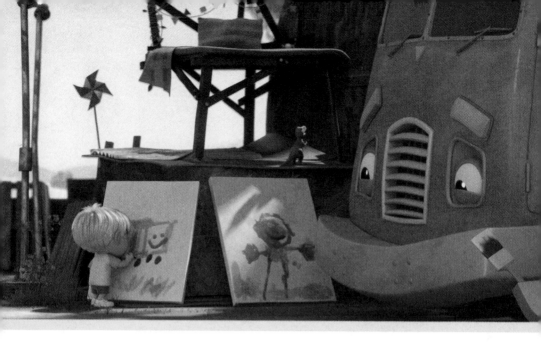

Hank and Trash Truck
do everything together.

They like to paint, ride bikes, and go to the Tree Fort. That's where they meet their friends.

This is Walter and Donny.

Walter is a sweet bear.

Donny is a curious raccoon.

Walter and Donny do
everything together.

They love to dig through
trash cans, eat snacks,
and even take naps.

Hank, Trash Truck, Walter,
and Donny have lots of fun.

They love to laugh
and be silly together.

Hank and Trash Truck also
like to visit their friend
Ms. Mona.

Ms. Mona is a clever rat. She lives in a little house that Hank and Trash Truck made for her.

Ms. Mona enjoys taking her friends out for ice cream.

Everyone loves extra sprinkles!

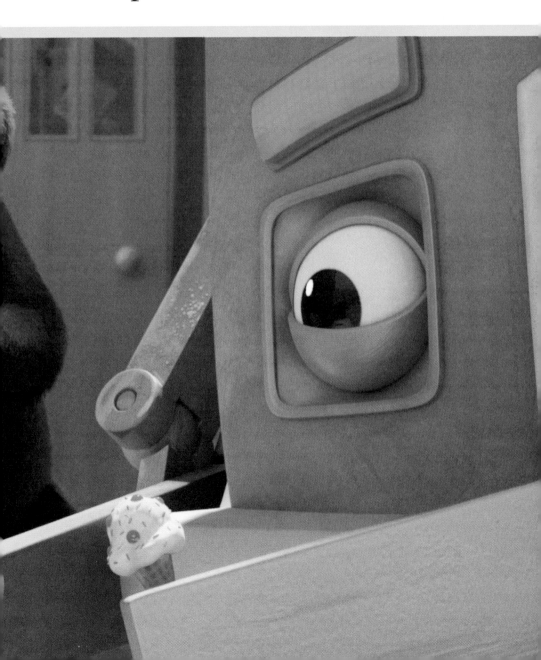

On special days, Hank's sister Olive comes to play.

Olive loves to dance and
teaches everybody how
to dance ballet.

One time, Olive and Trash
Truck performed together.

Trash Truck even did a twirl!

Hank, Trash Truck, Walter,
Donny, Ms. Mona, and Olive
love going on adventures
together.

Like surfing!

Hank and his friends
can go anywhere
they can imagine.

They can fly like a plane
and eat snacks
in Dream Land.

Hank and his friends'
favorite place to play
is at the Tree Fort.

But most of all,
they are just happy
to be together.

See you tomorrow for
another great adventure!
Honk!